FRANKLIN PARK PUBLIC LIBRARY
FRANKLIN PARK, ILL.

Each borrower is held responsible for all library material drawn on his card and for fines accruing on the same. No material will be issued until such fine has been paid.

All injuries to library material beyond reasonable wear and all losses shall be made good to the satisfaction of the Librarian.

Replacement costs will be billed after 42 days overdue.

Princess Candy

THE GREEN QUEEN OF MEAN

FRANKLIN PARK LIBRARY
FRANKLIN PARK, IL

STONE ARCH BOOKS
a capstone imprint

PRINCESS CANDY

THE GREEN QUEEN OF MEAN

WRITTEN BY

MICHAEL DAHL & SCOTT NICKEL

ILLUSTRATED BY

JEFF CROWTHER

DESIGNER: **BRANN GARVEY**   ART DIRECTOR: **BOB LENTZ**

SERIES EDITOR: **DONALD LEMKE**   CREATIVE DIRECTOR: **HEATHER KINDSETH**

ASSOC. EDITOR: **SEAN TULIEN**   EDITORIAL DIRECTOR: **MICHAEL DAHL**

PRODUCTION SPECIALIST: **MICHELLE BIEDSCHEID**

Graphic Sparks are published by Stone Arch Books a Capstone Imprint 151 Good Counsel Drive, P.O. Box 669 Mankato, Minnesota 56002 www.capstonepub.com Copyright © 2010 by Stone Arch Books All rights reserved. No part of this publication may be reproduced in whole or in part, or stored in a retrieval system, or transmitted in any form or by any means, electronic, mechanical, photocopying, recording, or otherwise, without written permission of the publisher.

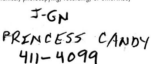

J-GN
PRINCESS CANDY
411-4099

Library of Congress Cataloging-in-Publication Data

Dahl, Michael.

The Green Queen of Mean / by Michael Dahl [and] by Scott Nickel ; illustrated by Jeff Crowther.

p. cm. – (Graphic sparks. Princess Candy)

ISBN 978-1-4342-1893-3 (library binding)   ISBN 978-1-4342-2803-1 (paperback)

1. Graphic novels. [1. Graphic novels. 2. Superheroes–Fiction. 3. Environmental protection–Fiction. 4. Schools–Fiction.] I. Nickel, Scott. II. Crowther, Jeff, ill. III. Title.

PZ7.7.D34Gr 2010

741.5'973–dc22   2009029808

Summary: The teacher, Mr. Slink, assigns an environmental project, and Halo Nightly pairs up with Flora, the school's resident tree hugger. Their team has the assignment in the bag (reusable, of course). But when the evil Doozie Hiss ruins their chances for a good grade, Flora changes from happy hippie to eco-terror. With her superpowered candies, Halo faces off against the Green Queen of Mean!

Printed in the United States of America in Stevens Point, Wisconsin.
122010
006037R

10

21

29

31

GREEN QUEEN

SUPER-VILLAIN

Villain Facts

First Appearance
Princess Candy: Green Queen of Mean

Real Name...........................Flora Fawn

Occupation..................Student, Activist

Height...........................4 feet 11 inches

Weight..................................77 pounds

Eyes...........................Cucumber Green

Hair.......................................Dirt Brown

Special Powers
Can conjure fighting flowers, clinging vines, and snippy Snapdragons. Flora has total control over all things Green.

Most gardeners weed their gardens, but Flora Fawn has a completely different kind of weeding to do. This tree hugger is trying to clean up Mother Earth, but not everyone wants to listen to her helpful tips for saving the planet. Anyone who doesn't heed this high-spirited hippie's warnings faces Flora's recycling rage, transforming her into the ferocious . . . Green Queen! With several vicious plant pets at her disposal, the Green Queen gives new meaning to the phrase "flower power." Enemies of nature beware – the Green Queen won't hesitate to turn litterers into plant food for her leafy minions.

AUNT PANDORA'S

PRINCESS PUZZLERS

Q: How long does it take a non-recycled aluminum can to decompose, or break down, on its own?

A: More than 500 years.

Q: How many trees could be saved every Sunday if everyone recycled their newspapers?

A: 500,000 trees.

Q: How many plastic water bottles are thrown into the trash every day instead of being recycled?

A: An estimated 40 million bottles.

About The Author

Michael Dahl has written more than 200 books for children and young adults. He is the creator of Princess Candy and author of *Sugar Hero* and *The Marshmallow Mermaid*, two other books in the series.

Scott Nickel works at Paws, inc., Jim Davis's famous Garfield studio. He has written dozens of children's books, including *Jimmy Sniffles vs The Mummy*, *Secret of the Summer School Zombies*, and *Wind Power Whiz Kid*. Scott lives in Indiana with his wife, two sons, six cats, and several sea monkeys.

About The Illustrator

Jeff Crowther has been drawing comics for as long as he can remember. Since graduating from college, Jeff has worked on a variety of illustrations for clients including Disney, *Adventures Magazine*, and *Boy's Life* magazine. He also wrote and illustrated the webcomic *Sketchbook* and has self-published several mini-comics. Jeff lives in Boardman, Ohio, with his wife, Elizabeth, and their children, Jonas and Noelle.

Glossary

brilliance (BRIL-yuhnss)—being smart

compost (KOM-pohst)—dead organic matter used to fertilize soil

environment (en-VYE-ruhn-muhnt)—the natural world of the land, sea, and air

fatal (FAY-tuhl)—causing death, or deadly

flash drive (FLASH DRIVE)—a small, high-tech device used to save and store computer files

organic (or-GAN-ik)—using only natural products and no chemicals or pesticides

pollution (puh-LOO-shuhn)—harmful materials that damage or contaminate the air, water, or soil

reduce (ree-DOOSS)—to make something smaller or less

thoughtlessness (THAWT-liss-ness)—if you are thoughtless, you do not consider the consequences of your actions

tree hugger (TREE HUH-guhr)—sometimes used as an insult against people who support protecting the environment

DISCUSSION QUESTION

1. At the end of this book, why do you think Doozie Hiss changed her mind about recycling?

2. Recycling aluminum cans is a good way to help reduce waste. What are some other things you can do to make the world a better place?

3. Halo has to team up with Flora for a class presentation. Do you prefer to do homework alone, or would you rather do group work? Why?

WRITING PROMPTS

1. If you could have either the power of wind, water, earth, or fire, which one would you choose? Why? What would you do with your newfound superpowers?

2. What would have been a better way for Flora to explain how important it is to recycle? Write a letter from Flora to a friend explaining why littering is bad.

3. Imagine that one of Flora's plant creations is out of control, and only Halo can stop it. First, draw a picture of this new plant monster. Then, write a short story about how Halo overcomes her leafy foe!